TWICE TOLD TALES

Twicetold Tales is published by Stone Arch Books
A Capstone Imprint
1710 Roe Crest Drive
North Mankato, Minnesota 56003
www.capstonepub.com

Library of Congress Cataloging-in-Publication Data
Snowe, Olivia, author.
  Dandelion and the witch / by Olivia Snowe; illustrated
by Michelle Lamoreaux.
      pages cm. -- (Twicetold tales)
  Summary: For fourteen years Dandelion has lived
in a house with the witch she thinks is her mother,
but when she shows signs of growing up the witch
locks her in a tower in the woods—where a boy named
Arthur hears her singing.
  ISBN 978-1-4342-9147-9 (library binding) -- ISBN
978-1-4342-9151-6 (pbk.) -- ISBN 978-1-4965-0084-7
(ebook)
1. Rapunzel (Tale)--Juvenile fiction. 2. Fairy tales.
3. Witches--Juvenile fiction. 4. Magic--Juvenile fiction.
[1. Fairy tales. 2. Folklore--Germany.] I. Lamoreaux,
Michelle, illustrator. II. Rapunzel. English. III. Title.
  PZ8.S41763Dan 2014
  398.2--dc23

                        2013045314

Designer: Kay Fraser
Vector Images: Shutterstock

Printed in China.
032014   8116WAIF14

Dandelion
and the Witch

by Olivia Snowe

illustrated by Michelle Lamoreaux

▼▼ STONE ARCH BOOKS™

You know the story.

You've heard it before.

Everyone has.

Now, read it again.

A new twist. A new gasp.

The story is told again.

TWICETOLD.

Jessamine Wood knelt on the cold tile floor of her apartment's tiny bathroom. Her feet stuck out the open doorway into the hall.

"Oh no," she said quietly.

Then she said it louder. Her moans of agony and dread echoed off the bathroom walls and floated out to the rest of the apartment.

Her husband, Bodhi, called from the

kitchen. "I can take the night off. They'll never miss me!"

Jessamine tried to reply, but she felt too sick. She heard his footsteps approaching on the creaky wood floor. "Don't come in here!" she said. "Please. Also, you can't stay home today. We can't afford for you to miss work."

Bodhi sighed, but he didn't argue. Jessamine hadn't been able to work in weeks. Without Bodhi's two jobs, they'd be out in the street.

Thinking about money made her sick again. She felt her husband's hand on her back, and, after wiping her mouth with the back of her hand, snarled at him, "I said don't come in here."

"Sorry," Bodhi said. He held down a glass of cold water. "I wanted to say good night. I'd better get going if I'm going."

Jessamine took the glass with a quiet thank-you and sipped slowly. "What time will you be home tonight?" she said. As the cold water rushed through her empty system, she felt a series of tiny kicks in her belly.

"I'm on till three," Bodhi said. "Franklin can't take his shift. His grandmother is dying."

"Again?" Jessamine said. She put down the glass and put out her hands so her husband could help her to her feet. Her head swam a bit as she stood. It always did.

"For the sixth time this year," Bodhi said. He kissed his wife on the forehead. "Get some sleep."

She almost laughed. She couldn't remember the last time she'd gotten more than an hour of shut-eye at a stretch.

Instead of trying to sleep in their stuffy apartment with no air-conditioning, Jessamine grabbed an empty paper bag from under the kitchen sink, slipped on her flip-flops, and followed her husband out into the night.

It was a ten-block walk to the discount movie theater. She didn't care what they were showing. She'd enjoy the air-conditioning, see as many movies as she could till the last one ended around two, and then she'd head home.

She'd done this before, nearly every time her husband had to cover the late-late shift.

Tonight the theater was showing an old animated movie she'd seen a hundred times. Still, it reminded her of being a kid. She stayed and watched the six o'clock showing, the nine o'clock showing, and the midnight showing. She cried the hardest the last time, even though she'd already seen it twice that night.

When the midnight showing was over, Jessamine was hungry.

The Woods lived in a busy neighborhood. Even at this hour, several businesses' doors stood open, letting their air-conditioning waft over the late-night sidewalks. Some of those open doors also released the scents of delicious-smelling food.

There was the doughnut shop at the corner

of Eighth Street. There was Mario's All-Night Pizza on Sycamore Avenue. There was the noodle shop at Fifteenth Street, just a block from Jessamine's apartment. Some nights, even inside with the windows closed, all she could smell was fish sauce and green onions.

But tonight, none of it smelled delicious. It was all she could do to hold her breath as she passed these places. She reached her apartment building, still gasping with hunger, but unable to think of a single thing she wanted to eat.

Standing in front of her building, digging through her huge purse for her keys, Jessamine caught a whiff of something. It was something familiar but exciting. It was strange and new but earthy and everlasting.

Dandelions. Their little yellow heads had closed for the night, but their greens, shaped like lion's teeth, grew like . . . well, like weeds all over the apartment building's front lawn.

Jessamine's heart pounded. For the first

time since she'd been pregnant, she knew what she wanted. She wanted dandelion leaves.

Before she knew what she was doing, Jessamine dropped her bag, fell to her knees on the front lawn, and grabbed handfuls of leaves. She put them in her mouth and chewed. They were peppery and fresh, sunny and cool.

She pulled up handfuls of dandelions as she went across the lawn, shoving them into her paper bag till it was almost bursting. Then she headed home.

Shaking with anticipation for the bag of delicious greens, she unlocked the building's front door. It always stuck, so she had to knock it with her shoulder. Then she hurried up the two flights of stairs to their apartment, made her way inside, and finally caught her breath.

She found the biggest bowl she could. She dumped the leaves in, rinsed them quickly under cold water, found a fork, and dug in.

2

Twenty minutes later, the bowl was empty, bits of green were stuck in her teeth, crumbs of soil clung to her lips, and she was still famished. Jessamine needed more. She stood up in the dark kitchen and went to the window.

Jessamine looked out into the apartment building's backyard, lit by floodlights to save the landlord insurance money, but with not a square inch of unpaved ground. A couple of dandelions had managed to grab a foothold along the fence on one side, but otherwise the backyard was bare, a lifeless slab of cement.

She could also see into the backyard of the next-door neighbor. She could see a small and bent tree in the center of the overgrown yard, undecorated and unkempt aside from a single ornamental scarecrow, scarier now no doubt, after surviving dozens of summer storms and hellish blizzards, than it had been when it was first stuffed and mounted.

Jessamine had seen these things before, standing at the kitchen's back window and looking out, letting the soothing steam from a cup of coffee waft up over her face on a winter morning. That was before she'd gotten pregnant, of course. She hadn't touched coffee in ages.

Tonight, she hardly noticed the tree and the scarecrow. Instead, her eyes slid over the unkempt yard and its beautiful yield: foot-high dandelions, each boasting leaves grander and more delicious looking than any she'd plucked from her own yard.

She had to have them. She grabbed an empty paper bag, opened the kitchen window's screen, and stepped carefully over the windowsill and onto the fire escape. The neighbor had no floodlights. Aside from that, she was something of a mystery.

Jessamine stepped carefully down to the second-floor fire escape. The window on that level was dark as well; normal people slept at this hour, of course, no matter how hot it was. Jessamine's belly barely fit through the opening to the ladder that led to the ground. Still, she squeezed through. "I'm sorry, baby," she muttered as she went. "It'll be worth it."

At the bottom of the ladder, Jessamine let herself drop to the cement patio. She headed for the decrepit wooden fence that separated the backyards and got on her tiptoes.

The woman next door was a mystery, yes, but one about whom the neighborhood loved to speculate. "She's the oldest woman in the neighborhood," they said.

"In the state," they argued.

"In the world!" they dared.

Unlikely, thought Jessamine as she went back behind her building and found a tall, sturdy garbage can. She dragged it toward the fence.

But that wasn't all they said. "She's still alive because of dark magic," they whispered.

"She's a witch," they said.

"She could kill you, you know," they threatened, "with a snap of her fingers."

Nonsense, Jessamine thought as she overturned the garbage can and carefully climbed. *There's no such thing as witches.*

Now she could see the whole of the next yard and the back door of the house. The lights inside were off. Surely even the oldest witch in creation would be asleep at this hour. Besides, it's not like Jessamine had any real crime in mind. She'd simply do some weeding. She was doing the old woman a favor.

Jessamine swung one leg over the fence. She groaned under the strain of pulling over the other leg and grabbed hold of the top of the fence to slowly let herself down. She dropped into a crouch again, a little less painfully this time, and immediately began picking up handfuls of dandelions and shoving them into her bag.

She was halfway across the small lawn, right at the foot of the scarecrow, on her hands and knees. Her bag was nearly full of dandelions, and so was her mouth. She smiled, the dark green chewed bits sticking out from her teeth, like she was some kind of madwoman. But she didn't care.

Behind her, something snapped, a twig or

a light switch, maybe, and she froze. Jessamine slowly turned her head and found the house still dark and quiet, the back door closed up tight. Even the windows were closed. *The old witch must have air-conditioning,* Jessamine thought. Then, from the darkness, a small form leaped at her.

Jessamine shrieked and rolled gracelessly onto her back as a black cat, its hair matted and caked with mud, landed on her chest. It hissed at her, its rotten mouth open wide, inches from her face, and Jessamine shrieked again. The cat bounded away from her, leaped to the top of the fence, and cast her a wicked look before moving on to a different yard.

Jessamine sat up and caught her breath. A light clicked on in the witch's house. Jessamine grabbed her bag of weeds and climbed to her feet. It wasn't easy. Even more troubling, though: she had no idea how she would get back over the fence to her own yard.

I have no choice, Jessamine thought, and she ran for the gate to the front yard. She clenched her fists tightly around the rolled-down top of her paper bag. The gate's latch stuck a bit, so she stepped back and kicked it hard. The latch popped open and fell to the ground, and the gate swung wide.

The back door of the house creaked open. Light flooded the weedy backyard.

Jessamine ran into the front yard and cut across her building's yard toward the front door. Then it struck her: she had no keys. They were upstairs on the kitchen table.

"Who is that?" creaked a voice from next door. "Who's been in my garden?"

Garden?! Jessamine thought. Her mind reeled. She pounded on the front door of her apartment building. "Please," she shouted. "Let me in!"

"I hear you," the old lady called to her with a voice dusty and old, but in a tone singsong and lovely. "You'll not get away, pretty pregnant neighbor."

Jessamine gasped. The woman knew who she was. *She is a witch,* Jessamine thought, the idea rushing through her body like ice water. She pounded harder on the door. "Anyone!" she shouted. "Please let me in."

"Jessa?" said a warm and gentle voice behind her.

She spun as she felt her husband's hand on her shoulder. "What's going on?" Bodhi asked.

Jessamine shook her head violently. "Just open the door," she said, practically sobbing. "We have to get inside right now."

"Why?" Bodhi said, but he pulled his keys from his pocket and opened the door. Jessamine hurried in and pulled the door closed behind them, making sure it was locked. Then she ran for the stairs.

"Jessa!" Bodhi called from behind her. But she didn't stop. She hadn't moved that fast in

months. In seconds, she was at their apartment door, drumming her palms on her thighs, wishing her husband could keep up. When he unlocked the door, Jessamine shoved it open, pulled Bodhi inside, and slammed it closed. She locked the bolt, put on the chain, and crouched against the door.

"Shh," she hissed at Bodhi.

"I'll just turn on some lights," he said, but she grabbed his arm.

"Don't!" she snapped. "She's watching us."

"Who?!" Bodhi said.

Jessamine looked into her husband's face, filled with care and confusion, and she realized what she'd done. Her hand went to her mouth. "Oh, Bodhi," she said, falling against his chest. "I've been a madwoman."

"Tell me what happened," he said, and she did. By the time she was done, both of them were crying with laughter, sitting together on the floor in front of the door.

"Then . . . then," Jessamine said, wiping the back of her hand across her eyes, "you showed up. 'What's going on?!'" She did her best deep-voice Bodhi impression.

"You should have seen you!" Bodhi said, smiling big. "You looked like—"

"A crazy person?" Jessamine said.

Bodhi nodded. "Exactly," he said. They smiled at each other. "We should try to sleep," Bodhi said. He stood up and offered his hands to his wife.

She groaned as she rose and said, "You know, I think I might sleep tonight. I feel . . . settled."

Together, they walked to the bedroom, Bodhi with his arm around his wife's waist, and Jessamine with her hands on her swelling belly.

~3~

For several nights, Jessamine and Bodhi slept well. He thought it was because of the cooler nights, as the temperature after midnight dropped below eighty for the first time in weeks. Jessamine, though, thought it was because of the dandelion leaves.

"I was craving something, and I got it," she said at bedtime early the next week. "Now my body can finally and truly relax and shut down at bedtime."

Bodhi watched his wife roll to her side and hug a pillow. She had three pillows in the bed now. It took that many to hold her body just so. Lying down comfortably wasn't easy for a woman who was pregnant. Only when he knew she was asleep—her breathing slow, a snore like a babbling brook rising up from her open mouth—did Bodhi shut his eyes and let sleep take him as well.

Hours later, he woke with a start. It was still dark. The clock shined red numerals at him. It wasn't yet four in the morning. Something had woken him, though. Bodhi reached across the bed and found the sheets empty and cold.

"Jessa?" he said quietly. There was no reply. He sat up and found the switch for the lamp, but as he touched it, something crashed in the kitchen. He left the lamp off and got up.

As quietly as he could, Bodhi moved down the short, narrow hallway. A light was on in the kitchen—the one over the stove. There came another crash of a bowl or plate falling and smashing against the counter.

Bodhi jumped around the corner, into the kitchen, and found his wife. She was up on the counter, on her knees, digging madly through the cupboard, tossing things to the floor as she rummaged. A mess of flour, rice, bruised apples, smashed plates and glasses, and other kitchen garbage littered the counter and floor.

"Jessa!" Bodhi shouted over the noise. She didn't reply. She didn't even pause in her madness. It was as if she was sleepwalking. He went to her and grabbed her arm. "Please stop!"

His touch seemed to snap her out of her trance, at least partially. She twisted her body to look at him. "I'm hungry."

"I see that," Bodhi said. "Let me help you down."

She did get down, but standing there, with her hands on his upper arms, her fingers digging into him like talons, the madness didn't drain from her face.

"What are you hungry for?" Bodhi said, though he suspected he knew the answer.

She leaned close to him, so her lips were almost against his. "Dandelions," she said, her voice deep and breathy. The word made Bodhi shiver.

"You're serious," Bodhi said. She nodded vigorously. Bodhi took a deep breath. He pushed her hair, wild and yellow, back from her forehead, like he was soothing a child. "Let's go back to bed," he said. "In the morning, maybe you'll feel more like yourself."

She knocked his hand away, though. "I am myself," she snapped. "And I want dandelions."

"Honey—" he began, but she cut him off.

"The witch's dandelions," she added. "Only those. Now."

Bodhi could hardly believe this woman was

his wife, a good-humored woman without an ounce of violence in her heart. Now, standing here with her, he thought she might hit him.

"Don't you remember, Jessa?" Bodhi said. He used his gentlest voice. "Last time . . . the old lady next door? She scared you really badly."

"It doesn't matter," she said, shaking her head. Her wild yellow hair fell around her face. "Are you too afraid?"

Bodhi thought of that night, his wife's panicked face as she pounded on their building's front door.

"Then I'll go myself," Jessamine said, pulling away from him.

"No!" he said, grabbing her wrist. "If you feel that strongly about it, I'll go for you. Of course I'll go."

Jessamine sat down at the table and crossed her arms. She stared at her husband with wild, wide eyes. "Well? What are you waiting for?"

"I'll have to get dressed first," Bodhi said, and he went to the bedroom.

* * *

"I can't believe I'm doing this," Bodhi muttered to himself. He didn't go down the fire escape like his wife had, and he didn't hop the fence. With a canvas tote bag over his shoulder, he took his keys, went out the front door, and stepped through the gate. Its latch was still broken.

Then he dropped to his knees, sighed deeply, and began plucking dandelion leaves. He'd been at it not more than a couple of minutes when he spotted the cat on the fence watching him.

"Good morning," Bodhi said, still plucking leaves nearby the scarecrow's feet. "Do you belong to the mistress of the house?"

The cat prowled back and forth along the top of the fence, then leaped to the scarecrow's stiff shoulder to watch Bodhi more closely.

"I hope you don't mind," Bodhi said, putting his attention back on the dandelions. "Just taking a few of these weeds off your paws, and then I'll be on my way."

"I do mind, actually," replied a thin and raspy voice.

Bodhi looked up, convinced for a moment that this matted stray cat had spoken to him. When he realized the truth, though, his skin went cold. He looked straight up into the wide and living eyes of the scarecrow. It cackled down at him, and Bodhi fell backward from his crouched position. He stumbled as he tried to get up and run.

"Run if you like," the scarecrow taunted him from behind. "I know very well where to find you."

Bodhi, up on one knee and about to burst toward the gate, stopped himself. He caught his breath. Surely the scarecrow hadn't spoken. It was impossible. Bodhi had gone mad.

Whatever wicked virus had infected his wife's pregnant brain had his under its spell as well.

He almost laughed. Then he shook his head and turned around. The scarecrow, though, hadn't finished with him yet. It dropped down from its post. At first its footing was wobbly, like it might fall right to the ground in a heap of old clothes and straw. Quickly, though, it found its composure.

Bodhi saw, then, that this was no scarecrow at all. What he had first thought was a floppy bunch of rags packed with hay and held up with sticks, he now saw had a real nose, sharp and pinched. He saw it had real eyes, narrow and bloodshot, with centers that were almost yellow. It had hair, too, long and silver, tumbling from its head.

He also saw that it had hands, with crooked, knotty fingers. He knew this because one grabbed his wrist. This was no scarecrow.

This was the old witch herself.

"Retribution," she said, in the same raspy voice the scarecrow had used.

Not the scarecrow, Bodhi told himself. *It was the woman the whole time.*

"R-r-retribution?" he stammered.

"Payment," the witch said. She let go of his wrist. "You and your wife have taken bushels of my dandelion leaves." She got up on her toes and leaned close to him, so close he could smell food on her breath, and added, "You owe me."

"For weeds?" Bodhi said.

"*Stolen* weeds," she said.

"I can pay you," Bodhi said.

The witch stepped back and looked him up and down. "That watch," she said, pointing one spindly finger at his wrist.

Bodhi pulled off the watch. It wasn't much to look at, but it had been his father's. "It's not worth much," he said.

The woman shook her head, dismissing

the idea. She tapped one long black fingernail against her front tooth and squinted at Bodhi.

"Perhaps you'd like to think about this," Bodhi said, forcing a smile. He was desperate to appear calm. He wasn't calm, though. "I'll come back when it's more convenient." He backed away as he spoke, feeling behind him for the gate. To his surprise, though, he never found it. He only found tall weeds and the bark of narrow young trees.

The witch laughed. "Look around you," she said. "You'll not leave here until we've settled on a price."

Around him, the yard had changed. This was no longer a tiny, overgrown yard, hidden behind a pair of buildings. It was a thick forest, and the moon hung low and fat in the sky.

"Where am I?" Bodhi said. His voice shook.

"You're safe," she said, "for now. I'll release you when we've settled on a price."

"Please," Bodhi said. "My wife will be

worried. I've been gone too long. She just wanted to eat some dandelion leaves." He laughed lightly. "You know how women are sometimes. They have these cravings."

The witch's face seemed to light up as Bodhi spoke. "She is with child," the witch said.

Bodhi nodded.

"Then the child," the old woman said. "She shall be the payment." She turned away from him, waving her hand. The backyard shimmered, returning to its normal form.

"Wait," Bodhi said. He grabbed her wrist. She spun and stared at his hand, and pain like fire shot up Bodhi's arm until he let her go.

"We've settled on a price," she said. "Take your weeds—all you like—and go home."

"Not that," Bodhi said, unwilling to leave. "Anything but that." But the old woman was already heading back inside.

"Please!" Bodhi called after her as the door

closed behind her. From the top of the fence, the black cat hissed at him. Bodhi, his shoulders sagging and his heart heavy, dragged his sack of weeds through the open gate and back to his apartment.

★ ★ ★

"I don't know what you're so worried about," Jessamine said. She sat at the kitchen table, madly stabbing at the dandelion leaves with her fork and shoving them into her mouth. She hadn't bothered with a bowl this time. She'd simply dumped the sack onto the table and started eating.

Bodhi paced behind her chair. He could hardly believe what his wife was saying. Had she really lost her mind?

"It's not like she's just going to stroll in here and take our baby," Jessamine said through a mouthful of leaves. Dark green bits sprayed across the table. She didn't seem to notice.

"You didn't see her," Bodhi said. "Not like I

did." His heart still raced. "She really is a witch . . . or something." He dropped into the chair beside his wife. "We have to run."

"Run?" she said, her eyes on her wild salad, her arm still working, moving the fork back and forth between her mouth and the pile.

"Away," Bodhi said. He took her hand, but she only pulled it away to continue eating. "We're leaving this place. Leaving this city."

"Oh, please," she said. "And where would we go?"

"Anywhere," Bodhi said, sighing. He stood up. "I'm going to pack. Only the essentials."

Jessamine grabbed his arm. "Stop," she said. "There's no hurry. I'm not due till Christmas."

Bodhi sat again, reluctantly. He sighed again. Jessamine ate for a few more minutes, then leaned back with her hands on her belly. "Thank you," she said. "That was wonderful."

"You feel better?" Bodhi said.

Jessamine nodded, a big smile on her round and red-cheeked face, and stood up. "We should get some sleep," she said.

Bodhi nodded slowly. He was so tired. He could hardly keep his head up and eyes open. "There was something else," he said. His mind was unclear, like a fog had blown in and settled in his brain. "Something important."

"How important could it be at five in the morning?" his wife said. "Let's get to bed."

Bodhi stood and took his wife's hand. "I'm sure it was something urgent," he said, his voice quiet and weak. "I was going to do something. We were arguing about it. I think."

Jessamine squeezed his hand. "When we wake up," she said. "When we wake up."

The fall was mild and lovely. Jessamine's health was good, and the baby, according to the doctor, was developing perfectly. Bodhi was given a promotion at his day job, so he was able to quit his night job.

One morning in late November, Jessamine stood at the kitchen window, looking out over the cement back lot and the wild backyard next door. Three men worked to clear out the brush and weeds and ragged-looking little trees.

She called Bodhi to the window to look.

"Perhaps she moved," Bodhi said. "And perhaps the new owners are finally going to do something with that miserable yard."

Jessamine frowned. She didn't think that was right, but she wasn't sure why.

"I won't miss her," Bodhi said, stepping away from the window and placing his coffee cup in the sink. "She always gave me the creeps."

Jessamine frowned again. There was something about that old lady . . . but she couldn't quite put her finger on what it was. Come to think of it, she couldn't even bring a picture of the woman's face into her mind. She wondered, just for a moment, if she'd ever even met the woman. She felt a kiss on her cheek and then heard the apartment door slam. It was the only way it closed. A moment later, she gritted her teeth, dropped her mug of cocoa, and held on to the windowsill as if for dear life.

The baby was coming.

★ ★ ★

The labor was long. Bodhi stayed at Jessamine's side the whole time. Nearly twenty hours later, a baby girl was born. She had her father's pale blue eyes. She had her mother's little pursed lips, and she had a full head of bright yellow hair. The nurses had washed her and capped her head with a little pink and blue hat. Jessamine pulled it off, and the little girl's hair fluffed up like dandelion petals.

Then they remembered.

As Jessamine, her hair matted to her forehead, held her new girl against her, and as Bodhi knelt beside their bed, his eyes red and his chin whiskered, it all flooded back. It was as if someone had lifted the heavy curtains in a dark room, letting sunlight pour in.

Bodhi jumped to his feet. "We have to go," he said. "We have to run, right now."

"Swaddle her," Jessamine said, handing

the brand-new baby to Bodhi. "I have to get dressed."

Bodhi nodded and wrapped the sleeping child in a thin hospital blanket. Holding her against his chest, he stuck his head out the room door. His skin went cold before he spotted her: the witch, standing at the nurses' desk only a few yards away, holding a bouquet of balloons.

Bodhi darted back into the room. "She's here," he hissed. He pressed the baby into his wife's arms, her coat only half on. He grabbed their small backpack and Jessamine's big purse, and then caught his wife by the elbow and pulled her out of the room.

The emergency exit to the stairway was nearby. Bodhi, with one hand still on his wife's elbow, slammed through the door. Alarms shrieked. A red light flashed in the hallway. Nurses jumped up from their desks.

The new family of three rushed down the

concrete staircase, their steps echoing through the stairwell, along with the steps of nurses following. At the bottom, Bodhi slammed his shoulder into the heavy exit door, sending another wave of sirens and red lights into a frenzy.

It had begun to snow in the night, and now it came with high winds and blinding whiteness. Jessamine wrapped her winter coat around her baby and followed Bodhi into the blizzard. He reached the parking garage and the car first, the old gray hatchback Bodhi had been driving since tenth grade. Both of them wondered if it would start as he climbed in and cranked it once, twice, three times. Nothing.

Jessamine strapped the baby into the car seat and stayed in the back as her husband cursed to himself and thumped the steering wheel. "Come on! Start!" he shouted, and he brought down his fist on the dashboard. The car coughed and then roared to life.

The tires screeched on the dry garage pavement. Jessamine leaned forward as Bodhi maneuvered the little car down toward the exit. "Turn on the heat?" she asked.

He didn't respond. He gripped the wheel with both hands so his knuckles were white. The car launched at the gate, down and waiting for payment, but Bodhi didn't stop. Jessamine curled her arms over the baby and shrieked as they plowed right through the gate and into the blizzard. Bodhi found the highway, took the first entrance he could, and sped west.

★ ★ ★

"We have to stop," Jessamine said. She had to scream over the baby's crying. "She's hungry. She's wet."

"Not yet," Bodhi said. He kept his eyes on the road and his cramped hands on the wheel. The snow had stopped an hour before. The little car zoomed down a desolate county highway, flat and straight as far as the eye could see. On either side of the road sat snow-covered farmland, divided by strips of evergreen trees, tall and spindly.

"Please, Bodhi," Jessamine said. "There's no one following us. Pull over. I'll feed her and change her and we'll keep going."

He looked in the rearview mirror at the barren road behind them, and he might have stopped for his wife and daughter. But at that moment, lightning cracked against the road in front of them, sending chunks of blacktop in every direction and leaving a crater behind. From the smoky hole in the road, a huge globe of light began to rise. It hovered toward the car.

Bodhi slammed on the brakes. The wheels screeched, and Bodhi lost control of the car. It rolled off the road and landed on its side. Bodhi's head spun. He struggled to open his eyes, but finally saw his wife in the backseat. Her eyes were closed. Her hair was matted against a bloody spot on her forehead. The baby screamed, her little eyes and fists squeezed tight against the noise of the howling winds and booming thunder.

Bodhi whispered, "The witch." He reached for his seat belt. But he could hardly move. Through the windshield, he watched the globe of light burst. A woman hovered before him. Today she was not the same bent old woman. She wore a blindingly white dress that hung past her feet instead of patched together black and brown rags. But he knew: it was the witch.

"No," he tried to scream, but he could hardly make a sound. The witch moved around the car, opened the door, and grabbed the baby.

The last thing Bodhi saw before he fainted was the witch floating off into the nearby fields, the baby in her arms.

~5~

A fourteen-year-old girl stood at her bedroom window, looking out over the wintery fields of her Northern Minnesota home. That window was where she always stood to practice her violin.

"It sounds wonderful, Dandelion!" her mother cooed from the hall.

Dandelion smiled a little, as much as she could with the instrument against her chin and throat. It did sound wonderful. It hardly

felt like practicing anymore. She could barely remember when it wasn't fun, in fact.

Mother had told her stories, of course, about when Dandelion was a tiny child, with a child's violin, throwing tantrums on the living room floor, unwilling to practice even a second more.

Mother was patient. Always patient. And now Dandelion's talent shined as brightly as her golden hair.

"Your hair is as bright as the petals of a dandelion," her mother always said. Every evening, they sat together in the dressing room, and Mother pulled a brush through her hair a hundred times.

It had never been cut, Mother said, and Dandelion believed it. Her hair was long enough to tangle on her bed's footboard as she slept.

When Dandelion was six years old, she had gone to her mother, who was busy boiling something in the kitchen, as usual, and asked her, "Where's my father?"

"You have no father," her mother told her.

Dandelion thought of the families she'd seen at the grocery store in town. She thought of the stories she read in the books that filled the shelves in her little bedroom at the back of the house. "Why not?" the girl asked.

"You're far too special for a father," her mother told her, setting down the stirring spoon and placing a hand on each of the girl's shoulders. "I raised you, instead, from the earth. I planted a seed in the garden next to this house, and you grew up from the ground like a flower."

"Oh," Dandelion said, and she thought about her name and her hair that grew wild and yellow, and she smiled. She was a fairy tale.

"Now go and practice your violin," her mother said, taking up the spoon again. "You know I love to hear you play."

At fourteen, though, Dandelion had begun to feel that something was strange about her. She saw others her age, on the rare occasion that she went to Main Street on the weekends. A boy with hair like rough-hewn hay worked at the grocery store. He said hello to her once, and Dandelion scurried off, feeling her face go hot and red.

There was another boy she knew. He brought the newspaper. One morning, Dandelion was in the garden pulling weeds—all but the dandelions, of course—when she heard the paper *thwack* against the front door. She brushed the dirt from her knees and pulled off her gloves, and then hurried to fetch the paper for her mother.

To Dandelion's surprise, the delivery boy was still there, leaning on the corner of the house, his arms and ankles crossed, watching her with wide eyes the color of chocolate.

"Morning," he said.

"Good morning," Dandelion said, and she pulled her eyes away from his to look at the walkway she stood on instead.

"Look, if your mother's home," the boy said, standing up straight and moving toward her, "she owes for the last three months of delivery."

Dandelion looked up. The boy held out an envelope. He shook it once, like she ought to take it from him. "It's the bill," he said.

She bit her lip and snatched the envelope from him. Then she turned on her heel and ran for the side door.

"Mother!" she said, running into the kitchen, where her mother was at the stove, her eyes on a recipe book. "The newspaper boy gave me this."

Mother glared at Dandelion over the top of her reading glasses and put out her hand for the envelope. She tore it open with a fingernail, scanned its message, and then tore it up and dropped the shreds into the pot on the stove. She went back to her book.

"Where did you get that?" she said.

"The paper boy," Dandelion said. "H-he handed it to me." She remembered his rich brown eyes. She remembered his black hair, which fell at an angle across his forehead, like someone had cut his hair with hedge trimmers while falling off a ladder. Dandelion giggled.

Her mother faced her and pulled off her glasses. "Did he do something funny?" she asked. Her voice was rigid and deep.

"No," Dandelion said. She crossed her fingers behind her back. She always did when Mother was angry with her, even if she didn't know why she was angry.

"You giggled," Mother said. "A most unpleasant sound."

"Sorry," Dandelion said. "I'll get back to weeding."

"A moment!" Mother said as Dandelion turned. "I'll be canceling the paper at once."

"Why?" Dandelion asked, keeping her voice calm and gentle. But her heart sank. She hadn't realized it, but she hoped to see that boy again. In some part of her brain and her heart, she even planned to be in the front garden tomorrow morning to greet him.

Mother looked down at her. She cocked her head and gave Dandelion a cold stare with one eye. "First, there was the boy at the grocery store," Mother said.

Dandelion flinched.

"You thought I didn't notice how he made your cheeks flush?" Mother went on. "You think I missed the look in your eyes?"

Dandelion crossed all her fingers.

"And now the paper boy has caught your eye," Mother said. "Giggling. At your age."

"I'm sorry, Mother," Dandelion said.

"Sorry?" She flipped off the stove and closed her recipe book. "You're fourteen."

What did that have to do with anything? "Yes, Mother," Dandelion said.

"Well," Mother said like the word was a breath of clean air after years underground. "Nothing to be done about it. I have a plan."

"A plan?" Dandelion said.

Mother smiled at her. She seemed her normal stature again, with her eyes just at the level of Dandelion's. She patted the girl's head, smoothed some wisps of golden hair that had escaped from the girl's complicated braids and bun. "I'd better get to work," Mother said.

That was ten days ago. Since then, Mother had been keeping quite busy—not in the house as she usually was, but off in the woods, where Dandelion was forbidden to go.

Whatever plan Mother was hatching, she was hatching it out there someplace, and Dandelion was worried.

The witch stood by the river. It rushed through the strip of woods—a two-hour walk out the back door of her house. She could hear it from her kitchen. It spoke to her.

Sometimes it said things idly, like: "The fallen oak near the Harrison farm on Route 61 has finally been overtaken by fly amanita mushrooms. Go harvest them."

Sometimes it said things far heavier. It

told her things like: "Mr. Cole, at the bank, is struggling for breath right now. He's having a heart attack. He's dying."

This afternoon, as she'd walked from the house to the river, it spoke to her the whole time. "She'll betray you," it said, its voice bubbling and bright. "She'll throw herself at any boy who comes along."

The witch muttered a curse at the river and plodded along.

"Unless you lock her away," the river said, its voice now rushing and violent.

The witch smiled now, standing at the river, and held her staff over her head in both hands. She shouted in a language barely spoken in a thousand years. The earth around her rumbled. The river tossed and laughed with glee. Then the witch smiled and walked back to the house.

"Come with me," she said, standing at Dandelion's bedroom door. "Bring the violin."

"Where?" Dandelion said, already standing up and packing the instrument. She didn't disobey her mother.

The witch moved to Dandelion's dressing table and collected her hairbrushes. She shoved them into a bag and hurried to the back door.

"Mother?" Dandelion called behind her, but the witch didn't answer, didn't look back, didn't even slow down.

She heard the girl hurrying to keep up, her timid footsteps on the path behind her. The girl was always so timid. It sickened the witch, but she wouldn't have it any other way.

When the girl was beside her and keeping step, the witch said to her, "I told you, didn't I, that I had a plan?"

"Oh," the girl said. "I guess I hoped you'd forgotten."

"Forgotten?" the witch snapped.

The girl was as big a fool as her mother and

father had been, thinking she could commit any act she wanted, no matter how senseless, and go unpunished.

"I was stupid to think so," the girl said. "Obviously."

The witch nodded and hurried her pace. "We should hurry," she said. "It'll be dark soon."

Now the river screamed at her. It shouted maddening lies about the girl. It shrieked warnings to the witch. The witch growled at the river.

"Lies," she whispered to herself. "You're trying to protect her."

The girl coughed.

"The river is a greater romantic than I imagined," the witch said, laughing. Neither she nor the girl spoke again till they reached the woods that lined the river. It was quiet now, calm and bubbly, moving along like an old man on a summer night's stroll.

"That's better," the witch mumbled. She let herself smile and turned to the girl— her daughter. "I'm so pleased you're here, Dandelion."

The girl lifted her chin. She even seemed ready to smile. The girl hardly ever smiled anymore. Lately she was always red-faced or flustered, or stomping through the hallway or the garden, frustrated or stricken or wallowing.

"I need you here with me to finish the enchantment, you see," the witch said. She took her girl by the shoulders and led her to a flat rock on the river's edge. "Sit."

The girl did so, carefully gathering her dress. She only wore dresses, unless she was working in the garden. She laid the violin across her knees and looked up at the witch— at her mother.

Once again, the witch held her staff in both hands over her head. She turned her back on the girl and spoke to the sun, now close to the western horizon. She dug deep inside her to find the right words to complete the spell she'd worked on for so many days.

My child will be safe now, she thought as she spoke the ancient words. *And the world will be safe from her.*

The world itself must have agreed with her, because as the witch spoke, the earth at Dandelion's feet cracked and seethed. It shot up two roots, which grabbed Dandelion's ankles and wrists, holding her in place on the rock. In a big circle around her, more rocks pushed through the soil, shook loose of dirt, and rose up around her, encircling her and lifting her up into the sky.

The girl screamed. The witch couldn't hear her over the violent din of her enchantment, but she could see her gaping mouth and her eyes wide with fear. Soon she'd cry, too, but it was all for the best.

Everything the witch did, everything she'd

done for the last fourteen years, had always been for the best. Would the girl have preferred living in a stinking old building in a disgusting city with horrible, thieving parents and going hungry as often as not? And by now she would have fallen in and out of love dozens of times.

She'd end up just like her mother, the witch told herself as she watched the tower of earth and stone rise up from the woods. The spell was complete.

"Mother!" Dandelion called, and the witch looked up at her. The girl stood at the tower's window, her hands on the stone sill. Her face was dirty and bruised, with a fresh cut on one cheek. "What have you done?"

"My plan, daughter," the witch said. "You'll be safe there."

"From what?" the girl shrieked down at her. Her voice, shrill and panicked, sent an electric shiver up and down the witch's spine.

The witch shut her eyes and clenched her

jaw against her senses. *Weak, timid, and afraid,* the witch thought. *A few years in my tower will surely fix that.*

"Please!" the girl shouted down to her as the witch turned to walk away. "You can't leave me here!"

"You'll be safe there," the witch said. "Safe forever. You have your violin!"

The witch walked on, and she was halfway back to the house when she finally heard the sorrowful strains of the girl's violin.

7

Arthur Oak was fourteen, and he didn't care.

"Heading down to hunt for frogs again?" his big brother teased him as they finished their breakfast of microwave sausage patties and hard-boiled eggs. It was all the older boy knew how to cook.

"Don't worry about it," Arthur said. He popped his egg in his mouth as he pulled on his sneakers. "I'll be back in time for the bus."

"You'd better be," his brother called after him. Arthur pushed through the back door. "If I have to explain why you missed the bus, I'll kick your butt into the middle of next week!"

The door slammed behind Arthur, and in a few moments he was clear across their back field. The Oaks' property ended at the low stone wall, but Arthur didn't care. He hopped over it. No one owned the land that ran for about a mile on either side of the river. At least, no one Arthur knew about.

He'd been coming down here, sometimes in the morning, sometimes after school, sometimes all day on a weekend, since he was four years old. He'd find frogs, sure, but he'd also build forts, try to catch a fish, go for a swim—anything he wanted.

Arthur's brother had stopped joining him on these explorations years ago. He said boys in high school shouldn't be playing with toads. They should be learning to drive and getting girlfriends and playing guitars. But Arthur didn't care.

He jogged the whole way to the river. Before he reached the narrow band of woods that protected his stretch of the river from eyes up on the highway, he spotted it: a stone tower rising up just past the treetops on the far side.

"Huh," he said. "That's new."

But it wasn't new, not really. As he got closer, he could tell that the stones, green with moss and with no rough edges, had been there for centuries. Millennia, even. This tower was older than any building around here for miles.

"Why haven't I ever seen it before?" he said. He pushed through the woods on his side of the river and stopped right at the water's edge.

The river frothed against the rocks, spraying his bare legs even though the wind was calm.

Arthur stood at the edge, enjoying the feel of the spray on his legs. It was a hot morning, though already September. He looked up at the tower and wished he could get across the river to take a closer look. Arthur swore the river sometimes spoke to him, but today he heard something else. A new sound. A sound that didn't belong in the woods or on the river.

It was simple music. A violin, he thought, or one of those other things some kids in the school orchestra played that looked like violins of different sizes. It was very beautiful.

Arthur took off his shoes and socks and stepped into the river. For some people, the river wasn't safe. The river would grab hold of a body and pull it along, tumbling and tossing it with the foam, into rocks and around bends till the river spit the body out ten miles closer to the city—if the body was lucky. Otherwise it might be dragged out to the sea.

Over the last ten years, Arthur and the river had learned to trust each other. He knew it wouldn't take him on a morning this peaceful.

A little closer to the tower, Arthur squinted

up through the trees and spotted a window, but the inside was too dark to make anything out.

"But it's a person," he whispered. "There's someone up there playing music."

He put his hands around his mouth and called up, "Hello!" He waited an answer, for the music to stop. Nothing. He tried again. Nothing happened.

"Whoever it is can't hear me," he said quietly, shaking his head. "I have to get closer."

But just then, he realized he had to get back. "The bus!" he said. He hurried to pull on his shoes and socks. If he ran as hard as he could, he'd still catch the bus. Hopefully.

★ ★ ★

"What happened to you?" asked Jasper Steel when Arthur dropped into the seat next to him.

"What do you mean?" Arthur pulled up his shirt to wipe the sweat from his face.

"Are you kidding?" Jasper said. "You look

like you just ran over here from all the way across town."

"I was down at the river," Arthur said.

"Of course," Jasper said. "What else is new."

Arthur shook his head. "Today was different," he whispered, almost to himself. "There was—forget it."

"What?" said Jasper.

Should he tell him about it? Arthur wasn't so sure. The river had always been his, and now it had shown its greatest mystery of all: an ancient tower, haunting music.

Arthur turned and looked out the bus window as it rumbled down the road. "Never mind," he said. "Just another frog. A big one."

The other boy laughed. "You never change, do you, Arthur?" he said.

"I guess not," Arthur said. But he had the distinct feeling he just had.

Dandelion sat in her tower room with her violin on her lap.

It wasn't a bad room. In fact, it was exactly like her bedroom at the house, except it was at the top of an enchanted tower instead of at the back of a little country cottage.

Somehow, her mother had created this tower out of stones and the ground, filling the room with a bed and chair and dressing table just like the ones Dandelion had always had.

For the first few nights, Dandelion didn't do much besides cry and play her violin. She was lonely, confused, and angry. Before long, she was hungry, too. That's when Mother came.

"My dear daughter Dandelion," her mother called from below. "Let your hair down to me, so I can climb up."

Dandelion almost laughed. Using her hair as a rope to climb? It was ridiculous. She went to the window, her arms crossed, and let all of her anger seep into her words. "You must be kidding," she said.

"The braid will hold," her mother called. "Wrap it around the bedpost for extra support."

Dandelion sucked her cheek and stared down at her mother's big, silver eyes. Always a different color, those eyes. Dandelion's were always blue—pale and flat, as interesting as a big, cloudless sky. But not Mother's.

She's not normal, Dandelion thought as she sighed and went to the bed.

She wound the braid around a bedpost, as her mother had suggested, and went back to the window. "Now what?" she shouted.

"Now throw down the end," her mother said. "I'll climb up to you." She held up a small basket. "I have your lunch here."

"What is it?" Dandelion called down from the window.

"Your favorites," Mother said, pulling back the cloth from the top of the basket. "Chicken salad sandwiches and watermelon slices."

"No chocolate?" Dandelion said. She risked a smile, and her mother smiled back.

"Perhaps," she said, and her teeth and eyes twinkled. She pulled her free hand from behind her back and held up a big wrapped chocolate bar, the kind with toffee chips—the best kind.

Dandelion whispered an excited "Yes!" as she tossed the end of her braid out the window. It fell just long enough so that her mother could grab hold of the end.

Mother climbed up with the basket hanging from her elbow. The climb looked much easier to Dandelion than she thought it would be.

Of course, Dandelion thought. *Everything is easy for Mother.*

She took her mother's arm and helped her climb in.

"We'll eat," Mother said, straightening her dress, "and then we'll play." She shot her daughter a stern glance. "You have been practicing, haven't you?"

Dandelion dropped onto the bed and threw up her hands. "What else is there to do?"

Mother smiled at her, as if Dandelion's complaint was a minor issue, not as if being locked in an enchanted tower by a mother who was possibly a madwoman was actually anything to be upset about.

Mother laid a picnic blanket on the tower chamber floor and Dandelion joined her, sighing. Then she put out the bowl of

watermelon slices—they looked like little smiling upside down Vs—and the chicken salad sandwiches.

"You have your books," Mother said. She sat down on the blanket and placed a hand on Dandelion's cheek. "You have me."

"Not for the last three days," Dandelion said in a serious tone.

Mother stood up. "Really, darling," she said. "It's not as if you've never been on your own before. I've been busy. You must learn to keep yourself busy, too."

* * *

After they ate, Mother put the dishes away. "Now," she said, "let's play something."

"What should we play?" Dandelion said.

In response, Mother went to the window and looked out for a moment. Then she turned back to face the room and began to sing.

Dandelion recognized it at once . . . one of Mother's favorites. She never understood the words; most of Mother's songs were in a language Dandelion didn't understand.

Dandelion put her violin under her chin and began to play along. It was an easy piece for her, though her mother's part was erratic, with octave jumps and long holds of very high notes.

Dandelion kept her eyes on her mother at the window. The sunlight streaming in gave the older woman a golden aura.

When the song was over, Mother clapped gently, smiling at her daughter.

"Can't I come home?" Dandelion said.

Her mother frowned. "My dearest girl," she said, "this is your home."

~9~

Arthur visited the tower every day. When he had the time, he'd run down before the school bus came.

By the end of the first month of school, Arthur had found a way to cross the river, but it was too far upstream for rushed mornings. There was a little bridge, probably made two hundred years ago by some farmer who used to own the land all over this area. Somehow it still stood.

It was after school each day that he took the extra-long walk along the riverbank and crossed to the other side, then hiked back downstream to find the tower. He circled the tower, thinking he'd find a door—probably a locked door—and instead found nothing.

"Hello!" Arthur called up, his hands around his mouth. Surely the violinist would hear him from this close.

But no reply came. The violin kept playing, and when it stopped to rest, Arthur shouted again, but only silence greeted him.

"A ladder," he said. "I'll have to get a ladder." But how he'd haul a ladder down here from his house all by himself, he had no idea.

* * *

Arthur never told anyone about the tower or the music. He never asked anyone to help him bring a ladder there. How could he explain? He'd have to tell them *everything*. But more than that, he'd have to share his tower.

So he simply visited every day, often before school, and always after school. He'd cross the river and sit on a big rock at the tower's base. He'd watch the river and listen to the music.

One morning, a couple of older boys on the bus spotted Arthur running up the hill to the bus stop. "Where you been, Art?" they said, knowing how much he hated that nickname.

Arthur tried to ignore them and make his way past them to find a seat. But the boys blocked the aisle. "We know where you were," they said. "You were down by the weird old tower, weren't you?"

Arthur froze. Did other people know about the tower? Were other people visiting it, listening to the music, wondering who lived inside?

He'd never seen anyone else there, and he was there almost any time he didn't have to be in school or at the dinner table or doing his homework.

"What do you know about it?" Arthur asked, narrowing his eyes at the boys.

They laughed. "Plenty," they said. "We know all about the girl who lives up there."

A girl?

"And we know she's crazy," they said, "just like her mom—the old witch."

A witch?

"And if you keep going down to the tower," they said, leaning close to him and sneering like hyenas, "you'll go crazy, too." They stood back, crossing their arms, and added, "As if you're not already. Art."

Arthur snarled and lunged at them, flailing and grabbing. He knocked them to the ground, having surprised them so well. But a moment later, they had him in their seat on his back.

They punched his arms and legs and chest until the bus driver slammed on the brakes and broke up the fight. Arthur found a seat right behind the driver. When he got to school, he was sent to the principal's office. Arthur had never even met the principal before. He'd only seen him walking the halls, slowly and menacing, two feet and two hundred pounds larger than anyone else.

"Detention," the principal said. "All week. Beginning today."

Arthur did his time. He finished his homework in detention, but his mind was elsewhere. It was on the tower.

He wondered if those older boys on the bus had any idea what they were talking about. He wondered if there really was a girl up there. He wondered about the witch, too. He'd never seen a witch around, but he didn't get into town much lately.

Arthur took the late-late bus home. He dragged himself inside just in time for dinner.

By the time Arthur had done the dishes and shown his mother his homework, it was getting dark. He grabbed a flashlight, said that he was going for a walk, and headed for the tower.

He'd never been down there so late. The night sky was clear and cold and filled with stars. The river was fast and shining, frothy at its edges, so the icy mist caught Arthur's face as he crossed the bridge to the tower's side.

The violin music was clear and fast as the river. It even shined. Arthur found his rock in the darkness and sat down. It was cold, but he didn't mind. "The music will warm me up," he told himself. And he listened.

After a moment, though, the violin wasn't alone. A voice joined in. It sang a melody so haunting and so foreign that it made Arthur's skin tingle. At first, he almost enjoyed it. Though he didn't understand the meaning of the words, he thought he understood their feelings. They struck him in the chest, and he clutched his hands together. Soon he was crying.

But before long, the voice became something too powerful, too strange, too frightening to listen to. Arthur became angry, afraid, and breathless, and he had to get away.

He burst away from the tower, ran for the bridge, and didn't stop running until he was inside his bedroom with the door locked behind him.

He decided he'd never go to the tower again.

* * *

Despite Arthur's decision, after a few days it became clear the decision wasn't really his to make at all.

When he slept, Arthur's dreams filled with beautiful, strange images. Not pictures, exactly. They were just colors, icy ones and bright ones and sunny ones. If he had to try to identify what he saw, he might have said, "It's a perfect winter morning reflecting off the surface of a lazy, swollen river."

But it wasn't just what he saw that haunted him. Had he only dreamed of those images, he might have been able to go on ignoring them, and the tower, for the rest of his life. No, he also *heard* something when he slept. He heard that violin.

Arthur couldn't remember the voice at all— the one that made his skin crawl and shiver and had sent him running back over the bridge and over the fields and into his bed. But the sound of the violin refused to leave his brain.

When he slept, it was the soundtrack to his beautiful dreams. When he was awake, he thought he heard it from around every corner. It was the song that that seemed to leak from other kids' headphones. It was the song that escaped through the open windows of passing cars on the two-laner.

After three nights and three days of this, Arthur had to go back.

Arthur didn't even go into his house after

the bus dropped him off that Wednesday afternoon. He dropped his backpack on the stoop and ran down the field to the bridge.

"I hope she's playing," he said to himself as he ran, hardly realizing that some small part of him did believe those boys from the bus. He was halfway over the bridge when he heard the violin, playing a happy and complex piece, as if in a duet with the rushing river beneath him.

He found his rock and was about to sit down to listen when he saw a woman approaching the tower from the far side. Quickly, he ducked into a thick patch of briar, wincing at the scrapes and catches of the thorny bushes.

The woman stopped at the base of the tower and looked up. She was very tall, with silver hair reaching past her waist. The way the witch moved, it almost seemed like she was floating just above the ground, rather than walking or standing.

"Dandelion!" the woman called out, looking up at the tower window. "Let down your hair to me!"

Arthur watched the window. The music stopped, and a girl appeared there. She had eyes as big and blue as the winter afternoon sky. Her hair was yellow and bright. She wore a simple green dress, as if she'd dressed to look as much like a flower as she could.

Arthur gasped out loud as the girl unraveled her yellow hair and let it down like a rope to the woman at the bottom. If not for the river's rushing white noise, he'd have given himself away. As it was, he thought he saw the woman flinch, and he dropped deeper into the bushes and held his breath.

He sat there, listening to them play again. And again, the woman's voice, terrifying and exotic, sent shivers up and down his body. This time Arthur stayed strong, though. He sat on the cold ground with his arms around his pulled-up knees. He kept his eyes closed tight and his teeth clenched.

Arthur couldn't guess how long the piece went on. It could have been a few moments. It could have been an hour. When the violin and the singing stopped, he shook as if waking from a dream. A moment later, he heard voices.

"I don't want to stay up here!" said one voice, the younger voice.

That's Dandelion, Arthur thought.

"That decision is not yours to make!" the woman blasted back. "If you continue to argue with me about this, perhaps we should stop these visits for good."

"No!" Dandelion said, her voice now timid.

The woman laughed. "I thought your strong front was a lie," she said. "I'll be back tomorrow. I'll put the leftovers here for your breakfast."

Arthur poked his head out of the briar patch to watch the woman leave. This time she simply stepped off the windowsill and floated gently to the ground.

"She *is* a witch," Arthur whispered.

Dandelion ran to the window. "Please," she called after the woman. "Don't leave me here, Mother! Winter is coming," Dandelion said, nearly in tears. "I won't survive."

"You'll be fine," the witch called back in a singsong voice. "You'll be safe forever."

Arthur jumped up from the briar patch and ran for his house. He didn't know how yet, and he didn't know when, but he'd save that girl from the tower. He had to.

It was very late that same night, and the witch stood in her kitchen and stared into a simmering potion pot on the stovetop.

The witch didn't sleep. She watched all day and all night.

The witch frowned. Didn't Dandelion see? The tower was for her own good, not for the witch's. The witch wished more than anything else that Dandelion could stay in the house with her, but a girl her age needed to be protected.

And the world needed to be protected from her.

As the witch watched the pot, seeing all things at once, she became aware of the boy.

"I've seen this boy," she said aloud. "He lives on the hill beyond the river. He rides the bus with two dozen other dirty, foul little beasts."

"I know where you're going, boy!" the witch snarled at the pot.

She blasted from the kitchen and out the back door and flew toward the tower, inches off the ground. As she streaked across the snow, she opened her mouth and let loose a wild, deafening shriek.

Fair warning, young man, she thought. *Leave my daughter alone.*

The witch zoomed across the snow-covered fields. In moments, the river was in sight, and beside it, standing tall and stark, was her daughter's tower.

Daughter, the witch thought darkly. *She's never truly been my daughter at all.*

The girl's golden hair hung from the window. The witch soared directly inside. "Where is he?" she roared at the girl.

Dandelion sat on the edge of her bed. "Wh-wh-who?" she stammered.

The witch sneered at the girl. "Don't try to deceive me," she said.

She sniffed the air. The boy hadn't been in the room; that much was certain. She hurried back to the window and peered into the darkness across the river. A lone black figure hurried up the white-covered slope.

"There he is," she said, letting a sinister smile crawl across her face. "I'll deal with him later." She spun on the girl. "But *you* will be dealt with right this moment."

"Please, Mother," Dandelion pleaded. "I haven't done anything."

The witch grabbed the girl by the wrist and pulled her to the window. "You let your hair down to that boy!" she snapped.

Dandelion pulled her arm, trying to get away.

The witch nearly laughed. "Where would you run to, girl," she said, "even if you were strong enough to escape my grip?"

The girl cried and quit pulling, letting the witch lead her to the window.

"What will you do with me?" Dandelion said, sniffling.

"I will put you out," the witch said. "You've disappointed me, but it was my own foolishness. I should have known that raising a girl who wouldn't give in to these desires would be impossible in this world."

"Put me out?" Dandelion said. "Where?"

"In exile," the witch said. "You'll probably survive somehow, but you'll never find your way out of the woods. Before that, though, there is one thing I must do."

The witch pulled a pair of scissors from her sleeve.

11

Arthur stayed away that morning. For the first time in months, he was already waiting outside when the school bus rolled up to his stop.

That sound—the witch rushing toward him . . . he couldn't get it out of his head.

"I never should have gone back to the tower," he muttered to himself.

He'd run away, leaving the girl alone to face that horrible woman. It haunted his memory all day. He couldn't focus on classes. Every sound he heard seemed drowned out by that terrible shriek.

"I have to go back again," he whispered to himself on the bus as it rolled back toward his house.

From the peak of the hill a quarter mile up the road, he thought he could see the tower. He had to be wrong about that, though. He'd never noticed it from this point before.

Arthur hurried off the bus, dropped his backpack next to the house, and ran down the hill, his feet sinking into the fresh snow. He slipped and slid and almost fell over and over, but he didn't stop.

The bridge was icy with spray from the wild river. Arthur had never seen it so angry. "It's angry at me," he told himself.

He ran to the tower and was about to call up to the window when he stopped.

The girl's hair still hung down.

"I've come back!" he said as he put his hands on the hair. He glanced up the hill, in the direction the witch had come from the night before.

He heard nothing. He saw nothing. Could it be safe?

Arthur climbed. It was harder work than the witch had made it seem. He went hand over hand, unable to use his feet to help him, as they slipped from the frozen tower whenever he tried.

When he reached the window, Arthur was breathless and his hands ached. His palms stung from the cold.

But he made it. He climbed headfirst through the window and tumbled onto the stone floor.

"Dandelion?" he said, peering into the dark room. A figure sat on the bed, a violin in her lap.

"I've come back," Arthur said, getting to his

feet. "To rescue you." He hurried to the girl and knelt at her feet.

He wished she'd respond. He wished she'd play the violin for him.

But she stayed perfectly still. She only said, "Light." Candles erupted around him, circling the room in bright light.

Arthur jumped to his feet, and the figure on the bed lifted the violin and swung it at him. It struck his head, knocking him to the ground.

He looked up, dazed, as the figure stood. It wasn't Dandelion at all. It was her mother . . . the witch.

"I knew you'd come back," she growled at him. "Boys like you always do."

Boys like me? Arthur thought, pressing his palm against his head. It throbbed with pain.

"But I've protected her," the witch said, "and she's far from here. Far from you. Far from everyone."

"Where?" Arthur said, barely a whisper.

The witch grabbed him by the collar of his parka. "You'll never know!" she said, dragging him to the window. "You'll never see her again!" She lifted him to the windowsill. "You like to hide in briar patches?" she said. "You like to see what you're not supposed to see?"

How could she know? Arthur thought. The witch shoved him out.

"Briars!" she shouted from above as he fell. "Briars!" And from the snowy ground beneath him, bare winter briar patches, woody and covered in thorns, rose up to grab him, not to spare him from the fall, but to claw at his coat and his face. The thorns cut his parka to shreds as he tumbled. They scratched his eyes till he couldn't see.

Arthur slammed into the snow-covered icy ground and blacked out.

12

Dandelion lived in the woods, far to the north. Her mother, the witch, left her there. "The wolves will likely eat you, if you're not too skinny from starvation," the witch had said. "But perhaps they won't bother with you."

She was starving. It had been weeks, and Dandelion had been eating snow and the bark of trees. When spring came, dandelions came with it, and the girl gathered their leaves and ate them, laughing as she did.

"Ironic, I guess," she told herself, munching on the leaves, "that I can only eat the plant I'm named after." But she thought the leaves were delicious, and she was surprised to find they filled her up, as if she'd eaten a huge meal.

She felt so good, in fact, that she wished for the first time since her exile began that she had her violin. She felt like playing. She felt like dancing.

So she sang. She didn't sing the words or melodies of her mother, though. She sang her own song, with its own melody. She couldn't think of the words to sing, though, so she sang a song without words.

It was while Dandelion was singing, collecting dandelion leaves as she went, that she came upon a small clearing in the dense woods. In the middle of the clearing was a cottage, so Dandelion went inside. The table and bedposts were covered with dust. The hearth was cold and crumbling, unused for many years.

Dandelion moved in.

Her first night in the cottage, she had a strange dream. She was lying in her bed, staring at the door of her new home, when a figure, so bright and so green that she could hardly look at it, glided in. "Who are you?" Dandelion asked, sitting up.

"I am a wood sprite," it said, "and these are my woods."

"Should I leave?" Dandelion asked.

The sprite laughed, and its laugh sounded like the river beside the tower on a calm autumn day. "You are always welcome here," she said. "I have come to tell you that the witch who drove you here is not your mother."

Dandelion's head swam, and for a moment she thought she might wake from the dream. But in her heart she knew it was true.

The sprite kissed Dandelion on the forehead, and then retreated from the cottage, giggling like water.

⌐13⌐

Arthur, blind and cold, never found his way home again. He wandered the wrong way for two days and two nights. When he got to a town, he hoped it was the one from which he came—but instead he was very far from it.

"Please," Arthur said, grabbing strangers by their wrists as they passed him on the quiet sidewalks. "My name is Arthur Oak. Don't you know me? Or my mother or brother?" But the strangers gasped at his face and torn clothes.

After he'd lived on the streets of that town for many weeks, and the weather began to warm, one kind man brought him to the police station. There, he cleaned up and was given food and clothing.

"We'll find your family," an officer said, patting the boy's cold hands.

"Thank you," Arthur said. But inside he was sad. Though he wanted to find his family, he mostly wanted to find Dandelion. He wanted to hear her play. In a world without sight, it was the only pleasure he could imagine.

Activity surrounded him in the station. Phones rang. Reporters arrived to speak to the boy who'd wandered in the winter for so long. Arthur hardly noticed it.

But one thing . . . one distant, faint sound broke through the din. Arthur stood up and felt his way to the door.

A reporter put a hand on his shoulder to stop him. "Where are you going?" she asked.

Arthur could sense a microphone in front of his face.

"Don't you hear that?" Arthur said, smiling. He hadn't smiled in so long. He pushed past her, into the street, and the sound grew louder.

"It's music," he said, and he followed it.

Before long, he smelled pine trees and the decay of a forest floor. He stopped a moment.

"You shouldn't go in there," a cameraman called after him. The rest of the crowd behind him murmured in agreement.

Arthur didn't care, though, and by now, so close to the source of the song, he was beaming. He entered the woods, and the reporters didn't follow.

He walked for an hour, the music growing louder the whole time, the air growing warmer, and his heart growing larger.

Finally the sound was just in front of him. He smelled a fire burning in the fireplace and soup cooking. He cautiously moved closer and felt his way to the door of a small cottage.

Arthur knocked. There was no response. But the music was coming from inside. He knocked again, louder this time, and the music stopped. He heard steps on the soft floor inside.

The door creaked open. A girl gasped.

"It's you, isn't it?" the girl said.

Arthur nodded.

"What has she done to you?" Dandelion asked, taking his hand and leading him inside.

"It doesn't matter," he said. "Please keep singing."

Dandelion led him to the fire. "Sit next to me," she said. "I don't know your name."

"I'm Arthur Oak," he said.

"Sit next to me, Arthur Oak," Dandelion said, so he did. Dandelion put an arm around Arthur's shoulders and he leaned against her, shivering, and Dandelion sang.

Rapunzel

• ★ • ★ •

Rapunzel is a German fairy tale that was published in 1812 by the Brothers Grimm, but some people think the story has older origins. Persian folklore produced a similar story, "Rudaba," in the 10th century.

Rapunzel begins when a pregnant woman craves rapunzel plants, which she can only find in a witch's garden. Her husband gathers the plant, but the witch accuses him of theft. The witch agrees to let them go free if they promise to give up their unborn child to her.

The witch raises the girl and names her Rapunzel. She grows up to be a beautiful young woman, with long, golden hair. When Rapunzel turns twelve, the witch locks her in a tower in the forest. When the witch visits, she orders Rapunzel to let down her long hair so she can climb up.

A young prince begins visiting Rapunzel secretly, also climbing her braid to the tower. Rapunzel discovers she is pregnant, and when the witch finds out, she cuts Rapunzel's braid and banishes her to the forest where, months later, she gives birth to twins.

The witch hangs the severed braid from the tower and the prince climbs up, thinking it is Rapunzel. He is shocked to find the witch there. She tells him he can no longer see Rapunzel, and, upset, he jumps from the tower, landing on thorns that blind him.

He then spends months wandering the wilderness until one day he hears Rapunzel singing. The two are reunited. Rapunzel cries upon seeing the prince, and her tears restore his sight. They go back to the prince's kingdom and live happily ever after.

Tell your own twicetold tale!

• ★ • ★ •

Choose one from each group, and write a story that combines all of the elements you've chosen.

A girl with extraordinary eyesight

An emperor who has a pet owl

A young woman who sells handmade rugs

A boy who has magical powers

A journal	An old mansion
A piano	A log cabin
A lucky charm	A tent
A ceramic mug	A houseboat

A happy toddler	A rat
A handsome giant	A gecko
An angry fairy	A cow
A tired mother	A frog

A rain forest

Ancient Egypt

Washington, DC

The Arctic tundra

about the author

Olivia Snowe lives between the falls, the forest, and the creek in Minneapolis, Minnesota.

about the illustrator

Michelle Lamoreaux is an illustrator from southern Utah. She works with many publishers, agencies, and magazines throughout the US. She currently works out of Salt Lake City, Utah.